the caterpillar that couldn't

A story by
JENNY SULLIVAN

Illustrated by
FRAN EVANS

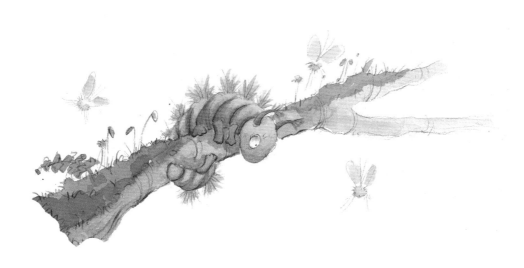

PONT

GW 2515879 1

KV-196-661

For my only "Sullivan" great-niece, Shannon,
and for my little friend Harriet Pritchard –
but Harriet, you have to read this to me!

J.S.

To Moss and Madge

F.E.

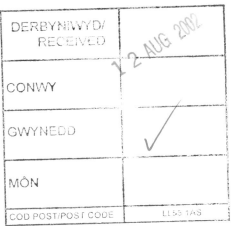

DERBYNIWYD/ RECEIVED	1 2 AUG 2002
CONWY	
GWYNEDD	✓
MÔN	
COD POST/POST CODE	LL55 1AS

25158791

First Impression—2002

ISBN 1 84323 071 2

© text: Jenny Sullivan
© illustrations: Fran Evans

Jenny Sullivan and Fran Evans have asserted their rights under the
Copyright, Designs and Patents Act, 1988, to be identified as Author
and Illustrator of this Work.

All rights reserved. No part of this book may be reproduced, stored in a
retrieval system, or transmitted in any form or by any means, electronic,
electrostatic, magnetic tape, mechanical, photocopying, recording or
otherwise without permission in writing from the publishers, Pont Books,
Gomer Press, Llandysul, Ceredigion.

This title is published with the support of the Arts Council of Wales.

Cover design: Olwen Fowler

Printed in Wales at
Gomer Press, Llandysul, Ceredigion SA44 4QL

Carwyn the Caterpillar was bored. There was nothing to do in his tree except eat all day.

'Caterpillars get bored, you know,' Carwyn complained to his friend, Owl. 'A caterpillar needs something to do.'

'Dooooo,' Owl agreed.

Owl scratched his beak and thought. 'If you eat your way to the end of that branch,' he told Carwyn, 'you will be able to see into the house next door.'

So Carwyn began to munch. He munched all
morning and half the afternoon, and at last he could see
into the house that stood just next door to his tree.

It was a big house. The sign over the front door read:

MADAME MORWEN'S SCHOOL OF DANCE

Through the downstairs window, Carwyn could see ten children all in a row, practising tap-dancing.

'All together now, one, two three,' Madame Morwen called. And ten children, keeping perfect time, wiggled their ankles:

T–t–t–tap–tap–tap

T–t–t–tap–tap–tap

T–t–t–tap

T–t–t–tap

T–t–t–TAP–TAP–TAP.

'Ooooh!' breathed Carwyn. 'I wish I could do that.
What a wonderful tappety noise.'

He inspected his feet. 'But my feet are silent feet.
I couldn't possibly do that.'

Owl ruffled his feathers. 'It's my opinion,' he said at last, 'that a person – or a caterpillar – can do ANYTHING AT ALL if they really want to.'

'Too-oo-oo,' the collared doves agreed.

'Rubbish, rubbish!' the magpie snapped.
'Rubbishrubbishrubbish. Caterpillars aren't supposed to
tap-dance! Caterpillars are supposed to eat and eat and
eat until they get nice and fat!'

And then I gobble them up, magpie thought.

'Please forgive me for speaking,' squirrel said shyly, 'but I've had an idea. If Carwyn dipped his feet into the sticky tree sap, I could stick some hard nutshells to his feet. Then, he'd have tappy, noisy feet like the dancers, wouldn't he?'

So Carwyn dipped his feet in the sticky, oozy sap, and squirrel fitted the nutshells. They tickled and that made Carwyn giggle. But he stayed still until the gluey sap had dried, then rolled over and stood up.

At least, he tried. The nutshells were so smooth and shiny that they skidded off the branch, and Owl had to rescue him, twice!

Poor Carwyn had rather more feet than Madame Morwen's pupils. He kept tripping over one set while he tried to tap the others.

'It's no good,' he said sadly, 'caterpillars can't tap-dance. Owl, I'm afraid you were wrong.'

Next day, Carwyn climbed up the tree-trunk to a higher branch. He ate all morning, and half way through the afternoon. He ate his way right to the end of the branch.

On the second floor of Madame Morwen's School of Dance, twenty children were learning to disco dance.

'Oooooh!' Carwyn breathed, watching the children twist and turn and leap and squirm to the sound of lovely, crashy, bashy music.

'Oooh!' he said again, 'I wish I could do that!'

'It's my opinion,' said Owl, 'that anyone can do anything if they really want to.'

'To-to-toooo!' agreed the collared doves.

'Magpie,' Owl said, 'go and fetch some bright things from your nest, please.'

I wish that caterpillar would just shut up and eat, magpie thought, *until he's fat and juicy!*

But the Owl was Boss Bird, and so magpie did as he was asked. He brought a pile of shiny bits that had fallen off the young dancers' costumes as they hurried in and out of Madame Morwen's house. Then spider helped dress Carwyn up.

'Oh, look at me, I'm so beautiful,' sighed Carwyn.
'Beeoooteeful!'

'Beoo-oo-oooo!' agreed the collared doves.

But although Carwyn looked wonderful in his finery, when he tried to twist and turn and spin and squirm like the disco dancers – well, he tied himself in some terrible knots!

It took Owl, the collared doves, squirrel, spider and the magpie AGES to untangle him.

'You were wrong again, Owl,' Carwyn said mournfully. 'Caterpillars can't disco dance, either, no matter how hard they try.'

'Never mind, Carwyn,' Owl said kindly. 'There must be something you can do.'

'I hope so,' Carwyn grumbled, 'because I'm still very, very bored.'

Just eat some more, Caterpillar, magpie thought.

'Have another leaf,' he said, nudging Carwyn higher up the tree.

You're getting closer to my nest now, thought Magpie, smiling to himself. *Soon I shall eat you with a nice salad, or maybe some chips. And perhaps a glass of blackberry wine.*

Carwyn climbed up to the next branch and began to eat. He munched all day, all night, and halfway through the next day. When he had eaten his way to the end of the branch, he could see into the third floor of Madame Morwen's School of Dance.

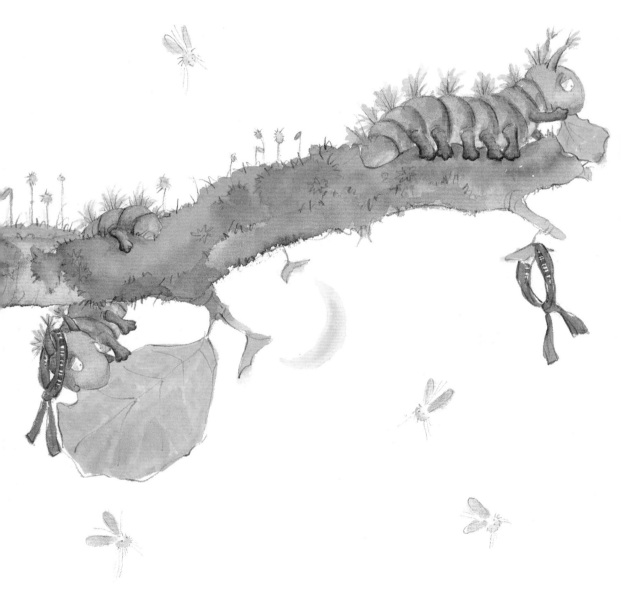

Five little girls, in tutus, were learning ballet.

They leapt and twirled and spun and soared, light as dandyclocks floating on the wind.

'Oh, oh, oh!' Carwyn breathed. 'Oh, I wish, I wish, I *wish* I could dance like that!'

'It's my opinion,' Owl began, 'that anyone can –'

'Shut up, please, Owl!' Carwyn said, putting his front feet in his ears. 'I don't want to hear it. I shall never be able to dance like that, not ever. I can't jump, I can't spin and I certainly can't soar or twirl. I'm just a caterpillar, and caterpillars can't dance. I'm fed up, I'm tired and I'm going to bed.'

'Chack! What a good idea!' said magpie. *Sleep and get fatter, caterpillar, sleep and get very fat.*

'Hooot,' Owl said humbly. 'I'm sorry, Carwyn. You tried so hard, but it seems that caterpillars can't dance after all, no matter how hard they try.'

Squirrel shook his head sadly and the collared doves cooed softly. Carwyn lay down on the branch and began to spin and spin until he was entirely wrapped up in his silky bedclothes.

He stayed in bed for a long, long time. Owl visited often, but Carwyn wouldn't speak to him.

The collared doves visited once, but they were in love and much too busy building a nest to bother with a caterpillar who ignored them.

Squirrel and spider came together, but when Carwyn wouldn't wake up no matter how hard they pleaded . . .

. . . they went sadly away.

At last, after a very long time, Owl decided that Enough was Enough.

'Hoooot! Get up at once, Carwyn. You can't stay in bed for ever, sulking. You're being very silly. Hooo-ooot.'

At last, Carwyn opened his eyes. He didn't feel cross any more. He had a strange, hopeful feeling in his middle, as if something wonderful was about to happen. He stretched, and his silky bedding ripped right down and fell apart.

'Don't care!' said Carwyn. 'I don't want to sleep another second. And I won't need that bed ever again.'

He crawled onto the branch. Some of his legs seemed to have disappeared, and something peculiar had happened to his body. Carwyn wriggled – and suddenly, over his head waved a pair of beautiful, jewel-coloured wings.

'Oh, look!' he cried. 'Look, everyone, look what's happened to me!'

'Hoooot!' said Owl.

'Oo-oo-look!' said the collared doves.

'Wow!' said squirrel and spider together. 'Wow!'

'Where's my lunch?' squawked magpie. 'Where's my beautiful, tasty, fat lunch gone?'

Carwyn waggled his new wings, just to see how they felt – and suddenly he was flying!

He floated and flitted and fluttered, and spun and twirled and twisted in the sunshine. He soared and swooped and laughed for joy.

'Oh, look at me, look at me, look at me!' he called, twirling and spinning and floating some more. 'Oh, look, look!' he said, looping-the-loop.

'Hooot!' Owl said. 'I was right! Anyone CAN do anything if they try hard enough! Look! Carwyn's dancing!'

And he was.